S.P. MISKOWSKI

THE BEST OF BOTH WORLDS

TREPIDATIO
PUBLISHING

ISBN: 978-1-950305-26-1 (sc)
ISBN: 978-1-950305-27-8 (ebook)

First printing edition: May 1, 2020
Published by Trepidatio Publishing in the United States of America.
Cover Design and Layout: Mikio Murakami
Interior Layout and Editing: Scarlett R. Algee
Proofread by Sean Leonard

Trepidatio Publishing, an imprint of JournalStone Publishing
3205 Sassafras Trail
Carbondale, Illinois 62901

Trepidatio books may be ordered through booksellers or by contacting:
Trepidatio | www.trepidatio.com
or
JournalStone | www.journalstone.com

"Miskowski peels back another dark layer of secrets in Skillute. Look if you dare. Family secrets are dangerous, especially when they're not yours." —Sarah Read, Bram Stoker Award -winning author of *The Bone Weaver's Orchard*

"Miskowski uses a deceptive slice-of-life to make a small cut, a little laceration to keep her story bleeding. Then she pulls and probes. In *The Best of Both Worlds* Miskowski spreads the wound of the Skillute cycle, showing a small community that won't stop hurting and characters who somehow are relatable and horrifying in the very same moment. The result is a strong, lacerating impression on the reader. This is a scar you'll remember." —S. L. Edwards, author of *Whiskey and Other Unusual Ghosts*

"To re-enter S.P. Miskowski's Skillute Cycle is always much like plunging head-first into a mad person's dream joined already in progress—something sly and malign by nature, perspective continually set askew, poisonous and hallucinogenic as a mould-laced 'shrooms trip and 'magical' in ways that would make any Disney witch puke on contact. Sitting slantwise to the action of her previous novella *The Worst Is Yet To Come, The Best Of Both Worlds* sinks us deep into the hidden-in-plain-sight lives of Pigeon and Roland Dempsey, passionately attached half-siblings whose adult lives have been spent carrying out anti-clockwise supernatural rituals designed to protect them against the sort of abuse which once bonded them together. But as the rest of the Cycle has already taught us, there's nothing in those dense, unforgiving Washington woods that wants to help anybody, no matter how much flattery and flowerbeds full of corpses you might offer it. This is brilliant, terse and beautifully dread-full writing from an author whose best just keeps on getting better." —Gemma Files, author of *Experimental Film*

THE BEST OF BOTH WORLDS

The dream of a drowned girl: *facedown with her braids lying, rope-heavy, draped across the nape of her neck; the sleeves of her gown patched at the elbows; her arms spread wide as though in greeting, and her eyes bright, open, gleaming underwater.*

Where is she? Pigeon stretches in bed and wonders how she can see the drowned girl's eyes. "Where am I?" she asks out loud. She doesn't notice when her arms and legs begin sinking, when she becomes a silhouette etched in sand. She falls asleep again.

She awakens to the call of wild geese. When she was a little girl, the unmistakable guttural honking seemed to her like people sobbing.

She's groggy from deep sleep. The season is wrong for north-flying geese. It's too early. She climbs out of bed and faces the window.

The flock is invisible behind a gray and violet swath of clouds. But the call, that heartbroken sound, grows louder. They're drawing closer. When they emerge from the clouds, their wings flash and turn to paper. Their feathers curl and singe; their smooth bodies plummet from the blackening sky. Their wings are paper fans swatting the air and falling away. Their calls are human voices, crying out a name over and over.

She knows she's still sleeping. But she can't interrupt her dreams, no matter how melancholy or frightening.

Roland, if he'd ever described his craving, might have compared it to an urge for teriyaki chicken. No matter how much he liked teriyaki chicken, he could forget about it for long periods of time, and it wasn't something he wanted for every meal. But once he felt the urge, once he acknowledged it and called it "teriyaki chicken," nothing else could satisfy his appetite. He knew it. He had tried all kinds of substitutions. Everything had failed.

His craving was funny in that same way, a random and unpredictable thing. He might not feel it for days, or for weeks. Then, all of a sudden, he could barely think of anything else.

On an overcast early spring day, following an uncharacteristic shopping spree at the mall, Roland was loading the Durango with bathroom accessories and thinking how much his sister, Pigeon, would enjoy redecorating. He scanned the parking lot and noticed a blue Acura, as clean and shiny as a new nickel. In the backseat were twin boys, maybe seven years old, watching movies.

Roland had to shake his head and laugh at the idea of kids with expensive entertainment like that. When he and his sister were little, the old man used to lock them in the tool shed for the day whenever he went on a bender. If he had to run an errand, he'd leave them in the cab of the truck, any time of year, no matter what the weather was like.

Roland figured the current temperature was low enough to leave kids locked inside a vehicle, but it was a bad idea for all kinds of other reasons. He couldn't guess how long the mom or dad would be gone. It might be a while.

The Acura was parked behind the bed and bath supply store, on the delivery side, near a dumpster and a loading ramp. There were other cars around, most of them SUVs, but no other people in sight, not at the moment. This was the unpredictable part. Roland had parked here to save time and because he hated the traffic on the other side of the mall, facing the freeway, and not for any other reason. Yet here was the blue Acura when he exited the store, like a sign. Life was strange.

The skin on his arms began to tingle. This might or might not be another sign. He had to marvel, sometimes, at the mystery of it all. He'd never figured out the exact nature of the craving and how it worked. Was it a gut reaction, like a leap of joy at every unexpected opportunity? Or was it something buried deep inside of him wanting to escape, always on the lookout for an excuse? Was it born when he was born, or did it creep inside when he was unaware, and make itself at home, and wait?

The twins stared at TV screens attached to the headrests in front of them. Without the screens they could have been asleep, or drugged, or hypnotized. They sat so still and silent.

After a minute one of the boys unlocked his door, left it ajar, and climbed out. He told his brother, inside the vehicle, he'd be right back: the one thing his parents must've warned him not to do whenever they were gone, not under any circumstance. He walked to the dumpster and stood on tiptoe to toss in some paper cups and candy wrappers.

Parents didn't scare their children enough nowadays, not in the right way. They needed to be scared once in a while. Kids couldn't figure out how to stay alive, especially these new ones from the city, with parents who moved here to keep them safe. These kids were crybabies, swaddled in cotton, never learning a hard lesson on their own, which was the only way to remember it—the icicle piercing the scalp when it fell, the shard of glass cutting a flared seam in the skin.

Roland's appetite expanded, opening a bright space between his ribs and his throat. At the same time, he was becoming bound to all the things he could see and hear and smell. Overhead the clouds shimmered, silver and anchor-gray, promising a drizzle of rain before the day was out. A light breeze carried the tart scent of barbecue.

These sensations were tinged with nostalgia. As much as he felt alive in the present, at these times Roland was acutely aware of the past as well.

Something had always been different with the land here in Skillute. His sister, Pigeon, had always said so. Third- and fourth-generation natives knew it. Not the newcomers moving in from Seattle and Portland, but the people who were born here. The old man used to sum it up by saying, "There's something in the water."

This explanation was only partly true. Skillute wasn't like any other town Roland had visited up and down the coast, although they all had a history, most of it bloody and mean. If all the people moving from overpriced cities to cheaper small towns knew how much blood had soaked the ground there, it would spoil their little fantasy of country living. Roland was sure of that. He was pretty sure something terrible must have happened in Skillute a long time ago.

In his hometown there were people who went out of their way to forget the past, both good and bad. According to Roland's sister, this was a serious mistake. Not paying attention, even if you chose not to pay tribute, was a mistake. There was a life—bristling, itching, not entirely human but not completely inhuman—in the dirt and the plants, and even in the air. It was there long before Roland was born, crawling along at its own pace under the soil. It was alive before the old man was born, if you believed the stories in their family. It was speaking underground, but only certain people could hear the words—people with a gift, a special talent. Pigeon tried to hear it. Sometimes she came close.

Pigeon's mother had named her Ava, but she only used her real name at work. Roland had nicknamed her for the cooing sounds she'd made when she was a toddler, a half-singing noise when she didn't feel like using words.

Her mother, Sophie, had been a Dodd by birth, and everybody knew Dodd women could speak to the dead. This was true of Sophie and the women in her family, which she could trace back more than a century, to the banks of the Columbia River and the forests surrounding Mount Coffin, and before that to a place called the Dering Woods somewhere in another country. Nobody could understand why Pigeon didn't have the gift as well. The old man had said it was a curse on Pigeon's mother for marrying him, a punishment, and maybe this was true. He said a lot of things when he was drunk, and he was drunk most nights and weekends. Once Sophie was gone, the old man stayed drunk more days than he was sober.

To find her rightful voice, to claim the gift that should belong to her, Pigeon had remained in Skillute and she would never leave, not even for a day. The place itself was alive, she said, and she aimed to understand it. She'd stayed through the bad years with the old man, and now she wasn't going to leave for anything. She thought if she kept at it, she was bound to break through. She was a determined girl, and she felt a calling deep in her soul.

Roland knew he had options Pigeon didn't have. He had no gift, and no legacy other than the old man's house and the surrounding fields. He could leave if he wanted. He could say goodbye to Pigeon and the home life they'd settled into after the old man died. He could walk away from his job, away from all he'd ever done and all that had been done to him in the old man's house. He could drive off and never come back.

But he didn't drive off. He was the elder sibling, and the stronger one. This made him the caretaker, the one who ran errands and picked up anything they might need outside of town.

Roland chose to stay, and he accepted the ways in which his choice set limits on his territory. He chose family over the greater safety and anonymity of the road. On those days when he stumbled upon an unlikely situation—twins left alone in a parking lot, for example—he felt the craving rise in his throat until he wanted to shout. He wanted to let loose and scream with joy. But he had to pick and choose. He had made a promise, to his sister and to himself, to pick and choose.

He didn't shout. He didn't scream. Not on that cloudy early spring day. He climbed into the driver's seat of the Durango and started the engine.

With his sister, the only woman he'd ever loved, Roland was part of a family, a real one. And every now and then, if he kept wide awake and alert, he caught sight of a stray, a loner with no friends to notice his absence, a passerby or someone with car trouble just traveling through the barely noticeable Skillute, a sprawling patchwork of old and new homes, a former lumber town washed up next to the freeway in the southwest corner of Washington state.

Any way he thought about it, he had the best of both worlds, right there in his hometown. He didn't want to mess it up. Once in a while he could afford to treat himself, but not today.

Pigeon was sweeping the house clean when Roland arrived, carefully guiding the dust and debris from west to east in each room, and then out the back door. She wore a butcher's apron to do her housekeeping. Her dark hair was wound in a loose bun. The pungent odor of sage lingered in the air.

She was pleased with the new shower curtain, towels, and bath mat. She tore open the cellophane packages right away, shook out the curtain, and hung it on a banister outside the back door to get rid of the sickening smell of plastic. Then she returned to the bathroom to open the other gifts.

"You just know these things are made for ten cents over in China some place," she said as she tore the tags off the mat. "Then the stores here jack up the price. That's how it works."

Roland stood watching her with both of his hands up, forearms resting against the doorframe. All the fancy stuff he bought matched the new tiles he'd laid during the winter. It gave him a warm glow to see how well he had chosen.

"Well, I can take all of it back to the store," he teased. "I'll just explain to the manager how we don't like Chinese shower curtains."

"No, you won't!" Pigeon clutched the bath mat like it was a bunch of roses. She could pull off high drama and a joke at the same time.

"The warehouse I worked at down in California, near San Pedro," he said. "All we did was take these vertical blinds out of crates from China, and load the same blinds into boxes labeled *Made in the U.S.A.*, to get shipped out again." He laughed. "That was the whole job!"

"One of the cooks at work, Arlene, used to have a job at a beauty salon in the mall," Pigeon said.

Roland leaned against the doorframe and crossed his arms over his chest. He liked to hear his sister tell a story, any story, even if it didn't have an ending.

"Sounds glamorous, right?" she said. "Well, she said it stunk. All she did was shampoo old women who were going bald, and answer the phone when the receptionist went to lunch, and sweep up all the hair from the floor. Now get this. She had to keep the cut-off hair sorted by color and length, because the gal who ran the salon sold it to a company that made wigs."

"You mean wig hair is real?" Roland asked.

Pigeon giggled. "Yes, it is, silly. Where'd you think it came from?"

She pushed past him and headed for the kitchen to start supper. He followed.

"Honest to God," said Roland, "I thought it was made in a factory, like doll hair."

"Maybe cheap ones," said Pigeon. She lit the gas range with a match and then lit a cigarette for each of them. "Leftover beef stew all right?"

He nodded. Beef stew was his favorite, and he didn't mind eating it two or three nights in a row. She cooked it the way his mother had. Then she poured it into containers and froze it. She saved them a lot of money with little tricks like that.

"But the fancy wigs, the good ones that cost a lot," she said. "They're handmade from real hair."

"It's kind of creepy, if you think about it," he said. "Wearing somebody else's hair."

Pigeon giggled again. "Yeah, it is," she agreed. "Rich women pay a fortune for a good wig, Arlene says. Well, the summer she worked at the salon, they had a *scandal.* Another shampoo girl stole a bunch of merchandise, gels and mousse and all, and she also took the hair the owner was about to sell."

"Took it? Stole it?" He shook his head. "So she could sell it herself?"

"Nope," said Pigeon. She stood by the range, watching the stew heat up in a cast iron pot. She took a drag off her cigarette and flicked ash into a star-shaped crystal tray on the kitchen table. Outside the window, two moths battered one another under the porch light.

"Rumor was," she went on, "the girl donated all of that hair to a charity for cancer patients."

"Well, that's a first," said Roland. "Stealing for charity instead of money. Have you heard of that before?"

"Not outside of a Robin Hood movie on TV," she said.

"What did she do with all the gels and mousse and whatever?"

"Oh," said Pigeon. She pondered for a second. "I don't know. I guess she wasn't all that good-hearted after all."

"You like what you do?" he asked. "You like Arlene and those other women?"

"At the cafeteria?" Pigeon shrugged. "It's all right. I'm used to it. The dishwashing's the easy part—sweaty, but easy. They've got a big washer with a conveyor belt. You've seen it. I stack the dishes and trays on these racks and start the engine. The prep work is just like cooking at home, only for hundreds of people instead of two."

Roland nodded. Now that she'd explained what she did every day, he realized he'd never asked her about it. He took it for granted Pigeon wouldn't do work she didn't like. As far as he was concerned, she could do just about anything. Her only limitation was her wish to stay rooted in their hometown.

"Middle school kids can be ugly to each other," she told him. "Most of their talk is mean, and most of them are pretty stupid. It isn't their fault. Their hormones start up and they've got no idea where they are, or what's going on. They pull dirty pranks, too. You wouldn't believe some of the things the head cook finds in the oven when she opens up the kitchen in the morning. One time it was a football helmet with a head inside of it, made out of meatloaf. Another time it was a whole dead possum family..."

Roland started to drift away. The comforting melody of Pigeon's voice soothed him, always had, and he recalled his own adventures when he was a boy.

Squirrel hunting was easy, but it wasn't much fun. For anything bigger, you had to obey the law and hunt during the season, and you needed a license. The day Roland found out there was no limit on crows if you caught them "in an act of depredation," he went wild. He killed about twenty of them and dragged them around in a burlap bag, until Pigeon found the stash and made him bury them in the garden, with candles and prayers in a ceremony she made up.

After that, Roland swore off killing birds. But he never got tired of stealing traps to re-set in the woods. Or pulling clothes off laundry lines and dragging them through the mud, or tossing rocks onto rooftops and into chimneys to wake up elderly neighbors in the middle of the night.

Most of his adventures could be called childish pranks. Outsiders might have applied another name, and his life could have turned in a different direction altogether. In some ways he had the old man to thank, the cranky old bastard who didn't believe teachers, guidance counselors, and whatnot had any business raising his kids. Thanks to the old man's views on education, any time Roland's pranks came to the attention of adults outside the family, the old man took it upon himself to solve the problem by taking him out of school. Punishment was a hunting trip, more often than not, where Roland was made to pitch the tents and carry the gear and not talk. He thought of this whole system as a magical loop from dumb misbehavior to outdoor adventure and back. He enjoyed all of it. These were the times when the old man was bearable, when he was almost a decent man hunting in the woods with his son.

Roland had trouble getting to sleep. The changing weather was hard to adjust to after a particularly harsh winter. The fragrance of the

9

early crocus, and the promise of a warm spring, kept him tossing and turning.

It seemed every thought of the day wanted to visit him again. No matter what else flicked past, the twins kept reappearing: their solemn faces turned toward Roland, the blankness of their expressions interchangeable, as if they were wearing masks. Their hair was neatly combed, and they wore matching button-down shirts.

They'd been taught polite caution, but wariness didn't come easily to children so coddled. They had no instinct for survival, and nothing they'd lived through had taught them what they needed to know.

The twin returning from the dumpster to his brother in the car had seen Roland and stopped. He was like a wooden puppet with oversized joints and flat, skinny limbs. The one in the backseat had turned. Both had stared at Roland, who noted the dash cam on the Acura. It wasn't pointed in his direction. He'd blinked, then, and caught a wavering fragment, a shadow at the corner of his eye, a moving object becoming larger, a figure approaching from the back door of the bed and bath supply store.

So he had called it a day. Tossed his keys in the air and whistled loudly when he caught them, exactly like a man with no bad intentions. He had climbed into the Durango and headed home. But the memory kept him awake that night, and the next.

The dream of starving women: *their white gowns stained with blood and urine, catching moonlight when they stumble through the damp moss and grass; they try to climb from a shallow stream onto the bank; their broken feet slip on the rocks and they sink to their knees in the shocking cold water.*

The shrill cry of an owl broke the night air. Black clouds puffed outward like the sails of great ships. Stray cottonwood fibers drifted across the yard, settling and rising, settling and rising. Pigeon couldn't recall another year when the cottonwood had appeared so early, not in her lifetime and not in any story she had been taught.

The dream of people moving through the house: *she can hear their footsteps shuffling, dragging, and a sort of buzz created by their murmuring, but she can't understand what they're saying. A woman brushes past her and her dress soaks with blood, warm and black-red, saturating the fabric. The woman is carrying a bundle in her arms, a dead animal wrapped in blankets.*

Pigeon awoke and reached for the candle beside her bed. By candlelight she searched the drawers of her nightstand for a small book handwritten in code. She felt, as surely as the wicked wisp of cold still winding through the early spring, that she must devise a stronger spell to protect her brother.

Roland's new interest started early one morning, purely by accident. He was driving to work with the windows down. He liked to breathe in the cool, fresh air, with a bite of Indian plum in it, after a night of rain. He spotted two girls—lanky, plain and pale, with messy hair.

Both of them looked like they were up to no good. For one thing, they weren't doing what they were supposed to be doing, which was heading for the school bus stop. They were doing something wrong when they first caught his eye. Talking with their heads inclined toward one, they seemed sneaky. And they strolled right past the bus stop.

Roland knew the driver: not well, but enough to wave hello and share a cup of coffee at school staff meetings. She was a laid-off computer programmer named Ellen, who pumped the brakes too hard at every stop and asked no questions. She wasn't paid to take a head count, she said. She was paid to drive safely in all weather, and make a brief stop at each designated waiting area. She wasn't a mom, she didn't listen to anything the children said, and she couldn't have guessed the names of the kids on her bus if her life depended on it.

The bus itself was ancient, repainted bi-annually. It was slow, and the fumes could be sickening in the back row, which all of the kids avoided.

This was one thing that hadn't changed since Roland had been in school. Pigeon had complained to their old man about the way the bus smelled, and he'd told her that was how the world was. It looked pretty through a window, but when you went outside, it got loud and ugly. If she wanted to live out there, she had to get used to it, he'd said. Then he'd made her get down on her hands and knees to scrub the concrete floor in the tool shed, so she'd remember the day she acted like a little princess.

Roland had seen the two girls before, walking separately, each in their own world. But they didn't make a strong impression until he saw them together. When they were together, something new happened, a strange chemical reaction. He could see it radiating around them. He was meant to see it, he decided. This was another sign, not part of the craving but something much bigger. It was the thing Pigeon was always warning him to look out for.

"It might be a way of walking or talking. Or it might be a kind of aura, or a color all around one person," Pigeon explained. "Or a funny smell. Or maybe something you can't put your finger on, but it keeps bothering you..."

"The way you tell it," said Roland, "it could be anything."

"Could be," she confirmed. "You notice a squirrel with a broken leg and it darts up a tree, dragging that hurt leg."

"You want me to bring squirrels home?"

"No, it's just an example," she said. Then she grinned because she knew he was teasing. "You might see it anywhere, if you really look. Let's say there's a flower bed full of red gladiolas, and right in the middle, you spot one stalk that's deep violet."

"Gladiolas come in violet, too," he said.

"It's not the color alone," she told him. "It might be almost any change. You might see it in a plant or an insect or a person. A difference will appear in one place, for no reason. It's like a flag or a marker. You see?"

"I guess so," Roland said. He wanted her to be pleased. He wanted the deep dimpled smile and the sound of her laugh.

Roland had noticed the girls by accident that day, walking together off campus, avoiding the bus stop. But then he remembered catching a glimpse of them running down the hall at school one afternoon. There had been no sign then, nothing to indicate they were different from all the other loud, messy kids he dealt with all the time. Both were yelling, or it had sounded like they were. Maybe their voices had echoed off the walls.

He just caught sight of them shoving a door wide open and rushing outside as he turned the corner, steering his cart out of the supply room. The girls didn't look back. They didn't hear him because he sprayed the casters of his cart with WD-40 once a week, to keep the wheels quiet.

The boy was sitting crumpled on the floor, and didn't notice Roland as he approached. Nobody ever noticed him. He didn't care.

It gave him peace of mind, being invisible right in front of people. He'd grown up here, had even gone to school here for a little while. This was one reason he got the job. Of course, he'd lied and said he'd graduated high school in Portland. He had papers and letters, most of them fake, complimenting and recommending his character and his janitorial skills.

When Roland thought about how busy and full of useless things the world was, he felt calm inside where no one could see him or hear the low, steady beat of his heart. Getting a job had been pretty easy. No criminal record, no arrests, no suspicion of anything. He just did as Pigeon suggested. He "fit the bill." He showed up and acted like the very thing they needed. He saved them the trouble of thinking about something they found boring and distasteful.

They needed someone to make the garbage and rodents go away. They needed shiny floors and magically well-stocked bathrooms. The school needed a man who didn't flinch while fishing dead chipmunks out of the swimming pool, their lungs hanging out of their mouths. Roland made it easy for the school to hire him and then forget about him. He did his job well.

Pigeon didn't have to lie when she'd applied for work in the cafeteria. She had cooked at a local restaurant for a few months. Before that she had cooked for the family for years, and if she could make the old man happy, she could do anything.

Silently, Roland wheeled his cart closer to the boy, who was crying and holding one hand cupped over an ear, whimpering like a baby left outside in the cold.

"You ought to go to the nurse's station," Roland said when he drew up alongside.

The boy gave him a look, one Roland knew well, sizing him up. Not for his strength, but for his value. What kind of house did he live in? How nice was his car? How much money did he have in the bank? Did he have a pretty wife, or an ugly one, or no wife? How much did a man in a gray cotton uniform with a nametag earn every week?

"Are you hurt?" Roland asked. "Did you get beat up?"

The boy shook his head. "Fuck off," he said. His words sounded thick, padded, formed with difficulty. Once he'd said them, he appeared to gain some courage. "Fuck off, you fucking re-tard."

This was how they were sometimes, before they knew their purpose. The boy and whoever raised him were perfect examples of the kind of people who'd been pouring into Skillute for years. Every one of them had a smart idea, and they thought their smart idea had never occurred to anyone else. Every one of them wanted more than the land could offer—peace of mind, or a fancy lifestyle, or a sense of security. They tried to take advantage of the place, to get ahead, to buy and own more stuff than they could afford in the city.

These people were never satisfied with life, and not being satisfied was a weakness. Because they would do bad things, or stupid things, to get what they wanted. They would make mistakes, like leaving their children locked in a vehicle, alone, watching a movie.

After the boy in the hall staggered away, still holding his ear, Roland took inventory. Counting his brushes calmed him. He checked the amount of cleaning solvent in his spray bottles. He wiped a smudge from the side panel of the cart. All was in order. He could complete his work plan for the day. The following afternoon he would haul out the vacuums and mops and the buffer.

"Crying like a whipped puppy," said Roland. "You should've seen him."

Pigeon dished up a mighty helping of macaroni and cheese. She was proud of the addition of chopped bacon. She took special pride in her one-pot meals.

"Was he a big boy? Looks too old for middle school?" she asked. "Barrel-chested, with light hair and a smirk on his face?"

"That about covers it," he said.

"I know him," she said. "Tyler Blanchard. He's a bad one. The head cook's complained about him a couple of times."

If Pigeon hadn't been able to identify the boy, Roland probably could have found out from the part-time secretary in the administrative office. She knew everybody. She was a big talker from California who wore too much makeup. Her false eyelashes made her squint and blink. She had a face like a cartoon character, and Roland couldn't help imagining hauling her slack body out of the swimming pool, water dribbling from her blood-red mouth.

But if he'd spoken to her, even a word, he would've had to listen to her complain about not getting enough hours thanks to cutbacks in the budget. It was all she ever talked about, besides her boyfriend. The guy was a construction worker, and he was laid off from his latest job. He watched TV at her apartment all day in his superhero pajamas instead of calling around for another job. She was about fed up with it, she kept saying, but she was still letting him eat her food and sleep in her bed.

All of this useless personal information Roland had learned while eavesdropping on the secretary and the shriveled office manager, who reminded him of a baby lizard. He'd overheard their conversation while mopping up vomit the day a student had taken a wrong turn while dashing to the nurse's station. By the time the girl realized her mistake it was too late. Cleaning up such accidents was one of Roland's duties.

He figured a casual comment about an unruly boy playing pranks, nothing serious, would have been all he needed to get the big-mouth secretary from California talking. She could go on for hours about any subject at all, sharing private information the way people did who had never been robbed or beaten. But he didn't like outsiders to know his special interests. As an alternative, it would have been easy enough to follow the boy home. Fortunately, Roland didn't have to bother with any of his usual tricks. He learned all about the kid from the gossip Pigeon had heard from her co-workers in the cafeteria.

The Blanchards, just the boy and his mother, lived in a brick colonial on a stony ridge lined with new homes. In that pretentious neighborhood the Blanchard house was the worst: big, fake window shutters painted forest green, and an antique livery carriage on the lawn. The description made it easy to locate.

A petite young woman wearing a black uniform with a white apron parked her old Toyota a quarter of a mile away, walked to the house, and let herself in with her own key. Must have been the maid or the housekeeper or whatever well-off people called them.

No wonder the boy was rude and foul-mouthed. He wasn't raised right. Probably had this young lady waiting on him hand and foot, cleaning his room for him, washing his clothes and asking if he needed anything else. Walking out to the road to the row of mailboxes, to collect the mail, when he was too lazy to do it. Hell, she probably called him "Mr. Blanchard." It wasn't a decent way to raise a boy, and he didn't deserve to be waited on.

Having satisfied his curiosity, Roland headed home. On the way he stumbled across a nice surprise.

"You think she enjoyed hitchhiking all over the country?" Pigeon asked. "Do you think she traveled far?"

"I expect she did," said Roland.

He examined the young woman's face in the amber light of the basement. She looked tired more than anything else. She'd seemed tired when she'd flagged him down near the freeway entrance, and more so when she settled into the seat beside him in the Durango.

Once Pigeon gave the signal, he rolled the young woman over onto her stomach on the stainless steel table. Naked in the soft light, she was both beautiful, with symmetrical arcs and curves, and scarred. If he had to guess, Roland would have said she'd been tortured. Some of the scars were faint, faded with time, but others might have opened anew with a little encouragement. She had golden hair, bobbed and loose. She wasn't Roland's type, if he'd been looking for a woman for sex, and besides, he'd already felt a powerful wave of joy and satisfaction when he killed her.

He watched Pigeon light the candle. She started whispering as she dribbled wax up and down the young woman's body wherever she noticed a blemish or mole.

"Allow this vessel to shield against harm..."

Roland didn't understand all of the words she used, but he loved the murmur of Pigeon's voice circling the body once, twice, three times. Then she signaled again, and he turned the young woman over to perform the same ritual on the other side, in the opposite direction.

When the ceremony was done, Pigeon leaned down and began to speak directly into the woman's left ear. The sound was like a breeze rippling across water. She stood like that, hunched over and whispering, for a long time.

Some nights Roland did nothing, just wandered around town in the Durango, remembering, thinking about what the town was like when he was a boy. Back then he used to imagine leaving Skillute for good. He thought about it all the time. He mapped out all the ways he might do it, and settled on his favorite because it was the simplest. He would walk to the freeway late at night, to hitch a ride with the first passing driver who would stop. He would ride to another town, and become a different person.

He kept this plan secret for years. It made him feel a little bit better knowing he might escape. But then his mother beat him to it by running away, and Pigeon's mother came to live with them. He was so young and ignorant he thought Sophie was happy, even after

Pigeon was born and the old man told Sophie she was stuck with him for good.

They didn't make friends at school, Roland and Pigeon. The old man claimed family was all they would ever need, and most people were shit or worse than shit. Most people would lie to your face and then shoot you dead as soon as you turned your back, he said.

That's what had happened to the old man, according to the legends he tried to create. His "business partner" took most of the money they'd invested, he said, and ran off with a waitress that used to work at an ancient tavern called the Blackbird, down the road from the lumberyard. The old man was convinced his partner would never have cheated him like that if it hadn't been for the waitress at the Blackbird, a tall, handsome redhead whose name was Dagmar.

On bad nights, the old man would drink hard and curse Dagmar for wrecking his life. He said if he could get his hands on her one more time, he'd break her in half.

His kids guessed the old man was directing at Dagmar's memory some of the rage he felt toward the women he had married, the women who'd either left him or died on him, according to the stories he told. He never spoke their names after they were gone. The old man referred to them in his own way.

"The absconded." The way he said it, with spite and a mouth full of phlegm, Roland and Pigeon were afraid to ask more.

They went on with their lives. They told everybody their mother was the same woman, and she was dead. Sympathetic to the point of sappiness, their teachers never once asked what happened to the woman who used to feed them and bathe them and kiss them goodnight.

This was Roland's first lesson in how easy it was for someone to fall through the cracks of the world without attracting as much attention as you might expect. It depended on a number of things, such as notoriety. Most people didn't miss what they'd never noticed in the first place. Another was popularity: not only how many people someone knew, but whether or not they liked that person as well as they claimed.

For example, Roland guessed Mrs. Blanchard would make a big stink about her boy Tyler if he disappeared, and then pretty quickly let it die down. He might be all she had, but he wasn't a very good son. Nobody would miss him very much.

The school principal and Mrs. Blanchard and the police would all discuss it, and decide he'd run off to Portland or Seattle to hang out with other bad kids. The news was full of reports on the drug dealers and junkies in both cities.

The boy would turn up when he got scared or when he ran out of money, they would say. And what if he didn't turn up? What if he was lost for good, vanished into nothing, picked up by chance and tossed to his fate over the rail of a ferry, knocked down by a car and left for dead, or knifed by a bum who wanted his shoes?

For the people who knew the boy, it would all amount to the same thing. He would be gone. He would never return. The absconded.

Roland and Pigeon had what the old man called "a decent upbringing." If hourly warnings about what a cesspool the world was, and frequent whippings with a belt or a birch walking stick were part of a decent upbringing, he wasn't lying. He doled out praise and punishment as he saw fit. He said Pigeon needed more guidance, since she was female and naturally disposed to evil. If he didn't watch out, she might turn into one of those lying bitches like Dagmar. Men were the ones who gave women direction so they could recognize their purpose, he said. Without men, they would go crazy. They'd run around making trouble.

When Roland finally decided he'd had enough, he didn't waste time. There was a busted-up Ford truck rusting away in a ditch. Only he knew about it. He got the truck running without making the old man suspicious. He hid a can of gasoline in the barn, with the parts he needed. As soon as he filled the tank with gas and replaced the battery and spark plugs, he rolled out of there and headed down the road.

The old man got worse by the day. He kept Pigeon home with him after Roland left. Some days he let her go for walks in the yard on a leash. Where they lived, there were no neighbors to see the starving horse in the barn, or the crying dog in the basement, or the girl on a chain walking in circles until she dropped from exhaustion. The animals died, but the girl kept living, some bright rage burning inside of her, waiting.

For a while Roland just ran. He worked at one place after another to get by. Convenience stores, gas stations, repair shops, and any crew where he didn't have to join a union. He'd stay a few weeks and move on to the next town. He couldn't afford to settle into a routine and start thinking. The old man had worked him hard for years, but he'd also taught him the skills he needed to stay employed. He was pretty good at everything he tried. He wasn't liked or disliked, just accepted and then ignored. His employers found him bland and conscientious. By extension, mistakenly, they felt he was trustworthy.

After a while the truck he'd used to make his escape died on him and couldn't be revived. That meant he'd be stuck in one place—oddly enough, an ugly nameless spot only sixty miles from Skillute—until he saved up enough for another vehicle. He tried to make a go of that, renting a room with a shared bathroom in a boarding house where most of the other tenants were alcoholics.

All of his nights were fitful. He dreamed about the old man, unchecked, left alone with only Pigeon to take his abuse. Roland couldn't stop thinking about it and how much uglier it must be, the old man's anger ratcheted up by his son's escape.

One night he couldn't sleep at all. He walked and smoked, and felt shame rise up in his chest. Every time he lay down and closed his eyes, he saw Pigeon's face. He heard her voice saying his name over and over, imploring him to come home.

Before dawn he ripped the license plates off a car he picked out from the parking lot of a ratty motel. He hot-wired it and drove just below the speed limit, all the way home. When he arrived, he cut the engine behind a patch of blackberry bushes and left the car there, where he could dispose of it later. He walked to the house, took off his belt and his boots, and climbed over the porch rail to avoid the warped plank that always squeaked.

He could hear them before he reached the bathroom at the end of the hall. Pigeon was talking to herself, saying the same thing over and over, like chanting or praying, to keep herself calm. The old man wasn't praying.

"Get on down there, now, where you belong," he said. "Get the sponge underneath and do like I told you..."

Roland would never forget the look on his sister's face—registering nothing, blank as a clean linen sheet—when he tiptoed into the bathroom with his belt in his hands. He wanted to greet her, but he knew everything now depended on speed. He reached down and slipped the belt over the old man's head, cinched it tight around his scrawny, wrinkled neck, and hauled him straight up out of the water.

Pigeon slung a rolled-up towel around the old man's ankles. She dug her nails into the towel and pulled down until Roland dropped the old man back into the bath. The soapy water foamed and spewed over the sides of the tub, and the splash drenched both killers.

This was how they knew they belonged together: not like a husband and wife, but like two animals that understood one another perfectly. Roland let the old man slip under the water. He just held him there, twitching, and allowed Pigeon to have the last pleasure. She yanked down on his ankles again and again, and watched his eyes staring up at her through the water, furious and terrified at the same time, until the spasms stopped and they knew he was dead.

They had the house. After the coroner, a pothead named Edison Franklin with an eight-month backlog of cases, confirmed the old man had used a belt to try and hang himself in the bath, apparently passing out with his nose underwater, Roland and Pigeon inherited the house and the land. All they needed was income.

He got the idea for his job from a late-night movie on TV. Young women kept disappearing from a college campus. A police detective followed lead after lead to a dead end. Then, one snowy night in the middle of winter, the detective also disappeared. No one was ever caught, and the bodies of the young women were never found. The final shot of the movie was a walk-in freezer, where the college maintenance man was storing the bodies.

Roland had never thought about doing janitorial work, but he possessed all of the required skills. So when the Clark Middle School maintenance guy went missing after calling in sick for two days, Roland applied for the job. He was better paid than he'd expected, but he did miss seeing his sister throughout the day.

A couple of months after he was hired, he read a notice on the bulletin board. The cafeteria was hiring part-time help. He mentioned this to Pigeon, who pinned up her hair, filled out the application, and signed her legal name: *Ava* (bestowed by her mother, Sophie) *Dempsey* (courtesy of the old man who'd raised her).

The two girls made trouble, the way Roland thought they might. They'd sure made trouble for the Blanchard boy, left him whimpering on the floor and holding his ear like a kindergartner. They must've realized there would be hell to pay, and they didn't care. This was what confirmed Roland's suspicions, after he had time to think it through: there was something special about those two, something strange and probably dangerous.

He spotted them every morning for a week, walking to school, holding hands like a couple. Maybe they were a couple. He couldn't tell. After lunch they liked to go to the school library together. He only had to pass the glass doors casually to see both lanky girls, sitting close, their heads bowed together. They almost looked like homely nuns, praying.

They wanted to bury the old man in his bathtub, naked, sitting up with purple-black bruises on his neck. They wanted to glue his eyes wide open.

Roland wanted to bury the tub and the old man up to the chin, with his head sticking out of the ground so the crows could play with his eyes. But Pigeon said he might try to spy on them, and they had to make the whole thing seem natural, so in the end they bought a pine coffin and had him buried in a cemetery like a normal person. As a final flourish, they'd planted red flowering currant on top of his grave, and left it to thrive or die.

"There," said Pigeon. "Now he'll help to give the winter hummingbirds nectar. In the spring the bees will congregate right here."

"He hated bees," said Roland.

"He did," said Pigeon with a smile. "And hummingbirds."

At home they took their time cultivating the garden. They were careful to include all of the plants the old man had complained about.

Roland tore up the bathroom. He threw out all the old fixtures. Then he built a vanity and put in a new sink and a luxurious bathtub with jets. He put up a shower rod, and installed tiles Pigeon painted by hand. But it was another month before she stopped bathing in a cheap aluminum tub and decided she was ready to redecorate. From then on, he made sure to bring home new towels and shower curtains and bath mats as often as they could afford. It was like a brand new revenge every time.

The day Roland went shopping for supplies, they were celebrating. He decided the twins had been a part of it, then, and not connected to his craving except to show him how strong he could be. Up to this point, he had been choosing people when the time and the situation were right. After the twins, he knew he could also practice a powerful self-discipline. This was good news to him, and he felt proud of himself. The hitchhiking girl had been a kind of substitute for the Blanchard boy, and also a gift.

He hadn't thought of his previous offerings in exactly this way. Yes, he had given them to Pigeon, and she'd performed her rituals on them. But he had chosen them for his own reasons, his own selfish craving.

Sometimes they fell into Roland's hands, and he almost failed to recognize them until he felt the space opening inside his chest. Once his body had confirmed the urge, and he did what he was meant to do, everything else happened naturally. As a bonus, in the spring their garden would be more beautiful than ever.

He was minding his own business, running an errand, when he noticed the UPS delivery truck parked on the shoulder of the road. He didn't see any other vehicles coming from either direction. This might be a sign.

He pulled over, but the driver wasn't paying any attention. The guy's head was bowed. He was deeply absorbed in his study of a paper map, comparing it to what seemed to be an elaborate navigation system. He didn't register surprise until Roland stood next to the sliding door.

The sandy-haired driver gazed down through his window at Roland, who then tapped lightly on the glass and waited. It was really amazing how trusting some people were. In this day and age, Roland thought, everyone ought to carry a weapon if they knew what was good for them.

When the driver opened the door to the cold air and asked what was up, Roland grabbed him by his jacket lapels and pulled him to the ground. Since there was no traffic at the moment, he decided to indulge himself right there in the open. He hoisted the guy against him and snapped his neck, then carried him over one shoulder to the Durango and tossed him in.

This one was what Pigeon called "a lark." Roland had felt the craving the instant he saw the young man's face. But if he hadn't taken time to pull over and check things out, he would have driven right past the opportunity. As it turned out, he had just enough time left on his lunch break to haul the UPS man home.

On the way, he noticed a strange abundance of cottonwood fibers in the air. He could only guess it was going to be an especially warm spring. Ordinarily they didn't see cottonwood shedding like this until May. It didn't make sense, but everybody said the weather was changing all over the world. The news was just one disaster followed by a worse one, every day.

Pigeon was home nursing a cold. Seeing the surprise change to delight on her beautiful face made it worth the effort. This was meant to be.

"Waste not, want not," Roland said as he strode through the front door of their house with the UPS man over his shoulder.

"You are kidding me!" Pigeon shouted happily. She jumped up from the sofa, threw aside her magazine and ran down the basement stairs to prepare.

"I've got to get back to work," Roland said after depositing the gift on the stainless steel table. "But I wanted to drop this off on the way."

With Pigeon standing in the yard in her sweatpants and a Seahawks T-shirt, waving goodbye with a Kleenex tissue, he steered the Durango back toward the road and headed to Clark Middle

School. He had done his duty, and Pigeon was pleased. It was a very good day.

He couldn't remember the substitute teacher's name. He checked the driver's license in her purse three times, and then gave up. It wasn't memorable at all. Mary Gordon or Marion Garner, or maybe Marie Granger.

On her last day at school, she just had to make one more trip to the women's room. A weak bladder was the sign of an over-sensitive nature, Pigeon had said.

Roland didn't follow the substitute teacher right out of the parking lot. He'd heard her griping about the long drive home to Castle Rock, and he'd seen her enter the bathroom. All he had to do was lock up his supplies, then head up I-5 in the Durango and take a detour at the first rest stop.

Sure enough, there was her car, and there she was exiting one of the little brick buildings. When she bustled over to complain that his vehicle was blocking her in, Roland apologized and twisted her head firmly to the right until her neck snapped. It was a method he had learned watching his mother kill chickens for dinner, many years ago.

There was the roly-poly store clerk at a tavern out near Coal Creek. The man wouldn't stop bragging about his gun collection, and how he'd shot at a homeless man he'd caught sleeping on his porch.

"Don't care what happens next election, it was all worth it to watch the snowflakes cry. Goddamn liberals griping about 'the little children in cages' and how sad it all is. I'll tell you what, if they had South American criminals pouring over the border into *their* backyard and trying to sleep on *their* porch, they'd sing a different song. They're all pissed off on behalf of the poor until they've got to pay to put the bastards up at a four-star hotel..."

The man went on like that for an hour. Then he rolled out into the twilight, started his truck, and headed west. Roland was waiting, having exited the tavern early to avoid suspicion. He followed the man all the way home.

This was a very special case. Not the craving, but genuine hatred. Maybe it was the man's voice, or the way he pronounced "MEX-ee-kanz" exactly the way the old man used to. Some familiar trait had flipped a switch, and Roland wanted to be the last person the man saw before he died.

He also wanted the man to die with birch twigs piercing his eardrums, for laughs. But he settled on the more mundane and plausibly accidental method of cramming half a steak down the man's throat at the supper table. He didn't take the remains home, didn't want the man in his house, didn't want to watch Pigeon whisper in his ear. Roland left him sitting there at his table, beer splashed on the floor and a piece of overcooked cow protruding from his mouth.

The actor was a fluke. Roland had never even heard of the Good Life Players. The anti-drug performances they gave at schools all over the state were highly rated, according to the big-mouth secretary in the office. Roland didn't ask. He just eavesdropped while turning in his timecard.

"They're the absolute best," Bigmouth told the lizard, "in our price range. I mean, the best available this time of year."

"Is this all they do?" the lizard asked.

"No," said Bigmouth. "I think they do Shakespeare on the beach near Astoria every summer. Or maybe that's another company.

Anyway, all of the actors are professional or semi-professional. They really know how to speak to these kids. It's *amazing*."

The following week, the Good Life Players put on a show in the auditorium. Dressed casually and using only black wooden blocks to suggest furniture, the six actors played scenes in settings the students were supposed to relate to—a classroom, a cafeteria, and a playground at a park.

"Hey, Sandy," one actress said to another in an unnaturally loud, high voice. "Why so glum?"

"Oh, you know," said the actress playing Sandy. "I'm kinda down since Kelly died."

A giggle and a groan broke out in the audience.

"Oh, right," said the first actress. "I know what you mean. Hey, tell you what will make you feel better." The actress took from her jacket pocket what appeared to be a joint, eliciting more giggles from the audience.

"Are you sure?" Sandy asked.

"Way sure," said the other actress. She took out a lighter and held it up to the joint.

Suddenly a man who looked forty or older, wearing jeans and an Ariana Grande T-shirt with a backpack slung over one shoulder, ran toward the others and shouted, "No, stop!"

"What's wrong?" asked Sandy.

"Don't you remember what happened to Kelly?" the middle-aged actor said. "He was my best friend ever, and he *died of a drug overdose*."

The actors clapped their hands once, to signal the scene was over. Their expressions became less serious, and they roamed around the stage. Suddenly one of them stopped and said to the audience, "What have we learned?"

Roland learned that the craving could occur anywhere, at any time. It could happen while watching a sketch performed by out-of-town actors who probably worked in restaurants or drew unemployment most of the year. This was both surprising and a little alarming.

When he cleaned up and decided to head home at the end of the day, his craving was confirmed. There, in the parking lot, the forty-something actor was smoking a cigarette and trying to reach someone on his phone. He leaned against a Camry so weathered it was impossible to say what color it had once been. The hood was up.

"Shit!" said the actor. He stared at the ancient flip phone. "Shit!" he said again.

Roland kept his stride to a normal pace on his way across the lot. He had time to assess the situation. A strand of cottonwood fell across his path and landed on the ground beside his left foot.

There were only four vehicles left, including the Durango and the Camry. The yellow Volkswagen with the bobble-headed Buddha on the dash belonged to the commie librarian, Mrs. Furillo. She'd be there all night, sorting her precious books.

The fourth car belonged to the vice principal. That was no problem. He would be working late, too, and then he'd head right over to the nearest tavern to get drunk.

"Hey," said the actor as Roland approached. He shifted his weight, and Roland could see large sweat stains under both arms.

"Hey," said Roland. "No smoking allowed on school premises."

The actor looked annoyed. He took a final drag and threw the cigarette down. Roland kept staring at the butt smoldering on the asphalt until the actor picked it up, put it out with his shoe, and deposited the remains in the Camry's ashtray.

"Uh," he said. "Sorry. I'm trying to call a friend and she's not answering."

Roland nodded. He was aware of the CCTV surveillance. Skillute wasn't state of the art, regarding security. The schools, the post office, and convenience stores were the places where cameras were most likely to pick up his activities.

"I don't suppose you have jumper cables?" the actor asked.

Now Roland smiled. His craving had been confirmed, and he felt the space inside opening like a window on a balmy day. "Sure do," he said. "Let me pull over here and we'll get you started."

The relief on the guy's face was almost comical. Automatically he reached for another cigarette, found the pack empty, crushed it and tossed it into the car. It landed on a pile of McDonald's paper bags, shoes, Styrofoam cups, scripts and clothes hangers.

When Roland gave his car a jump and a slight push to get him out of the lot and on his way, the actor waved goodbye but didn't look back over his shoulder. The whole thing took less than ten minutes.

Roland had no trouble locating the actor. He pulled the Durango off the road and waited about half a mile past the nearest convenience store, where the actor stopped to buy cigarettes and a large coffee. Then he followed until the actor stopped again, to pee on some shrubbery.

"What's this on his back?" Pigeon asked after they had stripped the bruised body in the basement.

Roland leaned down to get a better view. It would only be a matter of months before he needed glasses. He wondered if he could get away with a pair of those magnifying lenses sold at the pharmacy on a spinning rack. He squinted.

"That," said Roland, "is a tattoo of two faces. One's laughing and one's crying."

"Ooo," she cooed. "Well, that's something. What does it mean?"

"I don't know," he said. "Probably an actor thing."

"That's it!" she said. "You told me he was an actor."

"Yeah."

"I think I saw him in a mattress commercial on TV one time," she said.

They both stood back a bit and nodded, impressed. Then Pigeon lit a candle and let it drip onto the actor's lower back. Soon the tattoo was spattered with hot wax, and she began to whisper.

"Seal this vessel and make it as new. Allow this vessel to guard against evil…"

They were plotting something, but he didn't know what it might be. After the last bell rang, he watched the two girls sneak off together instead of riding the bus home.

He was beginning to think the scroungier of the two might be the strange one, the one setting off signals in his head. When he watched her move and speak, he remembered the violet gladiola Pigeon had used as an example. There was something wired wrong, or disconnected, or just plain crazy about the girl. Her hair was a mess, she wore shabbier clothes than anyone else at school, and like the actor the girl had a tattoo. Hers was ugly: tangled brown ivy up the side of her neck.

He spent some time studying both girls and where they lived. The signals were definitely coming from the scroungy one. They grew stronger and wilder when the two were together, but they originated with the scroungy one, who lived in the trailer park.

Roland considered telling Pigeon about the girls. He wanted to. Maybe they should discuss this feeling he had every time he followed them. It wasn't the craving, not exactly. It was new and confusing.

But what could he tell his sister? For the first time, he was afraid to take matters into his own hands. What was he afraid of, a couple of teenage girls? What could they do to him?

Truth be told, Roland had taken out some of his frustration and confusion on the actor. He'd also stolen his cigarettes. He didn't like to take trophies, as a rule. A trophy was a nuisance, and it could be incriminating. But since the cigarettes weren't going to last long, he thought of them in the same category as the clothing he burned in a metal trashcan.

Everything about the actor had been unusual, in an interesting way. Pigeon had the idea it might be easier to talk with someone after death if his last moments were filled with a strong feeling, like fear, and if his death occurred only minutes before the ritual. Roland suspected she'd picked up this idea from a movie, but he never questioned her methods.

So he had taken the actor home alive, ankles and wrists and mouth duct-taped. When the sun went down, he'd dropped the guy on the ground in the fenced section of the yard while Pigeon cooked supper and watched from the kitchen window. Roland had taken a seat on a lawn chair and watched the actor try to squirm free of his restraints.

First the guy started snaking sideways on his belly. He was no athlete. That much was obvious. No matter how hard he rocked back and forth, he couldn't get enough momentum to roll up onto his knees and stand, not without tipping to one side and crashing back to the ground.

After a while the duct tape on his face started slipping from all the saliva and snot. Roland brought a plastic bag from the kitchen and tied it over the guy's head. He made some noises like an injured pig, then, but he still couldn't stand up. The more he struggled, the more desperately he snuffled for a breath of air inside the plastic bag. Drawn tightly, it formed a second skin across his face. He made a gagging noise when he tried to spit out the tape, which had bunched up and gotten caught in his mouth. Panic caused him to scream, a muffled scream, but loud enough for anyone passing to notice.

Luckily, no one ever passed by. Not a lot of Skillute natives went for "fun walks" in what was left of the woods, or stomped around the countryside for exercise. Only the city transplants did that, and most of them figured out pretty fast how dangerous the landscape could be. There were half-built houses and leftover materials everywhere. Holes had been dug for foundations, and then forgotten when construction was abandoned. Wells had been leveled, but never filled in and covered. Then there were ditches and deep holes that once caught waste from outhouses. By law, these shouldn't have existed anymore, but you never knew what you might stumble upon. All of this was obvious and yet, every season, some new resident had to be rescued or rushed to the hospital after an accident.

The wriggling and fighting was all right, but the noise started to be irritating. Roland realized it wouldn't take much longer for the actor to die, but he just couldn't stomach the whole drawn-out death scene. He scanned the ground on either side of him and found a fist-sized rock.

"Show's over," he said, and slammed the sharp edge of the rock down against the back of the actor's neck.

The world was quieter after that. Roland could hear his heartbeat. It thumped gently, steadily. It felt good to be there in the cold shade of the surrounding evergreens, at night, with Pigeon cooking supper inside the house, smiling and singing a little song she'd made up about roses blooming in twilight. He decided to let himself enjoy these things for a minute or two, before he hauled the actor down to the basement.

The dream of a woman consumed by fire: *a gust of air through a door frame; the woman's black hair rising and spinning over her head like a cyclone; the tongue of fire licking her skin away.*

At some point Roland's targets usually made it into the news. There they competed for attention with stories of street and bridge repair bonds, efforts to stop drag racing in Rose Valley on Sundays, town budget cuts, power outages, barn burnings, drug busts, fundraisers to benefit animal shelters, and local businesses celebrating insignificant anniversaries to drum up customers. Lost in the all-equal news items were the substitute teacher who disappeared on the morning she was scheduled to begin tutoring a bedridden student in Longview; the unemployed stage actor whose car was found burned up at the bottom of a rock quarry in the next county; the UPS driver who had stolen valuable packaged merchandise and absconded, probably to avoid overdue child support payments to the ex-wife who was suing him.

Roland had long known that people judged one another's worth by income and influence. If any of these people had been wealthy, their disappearances would have made headlines for weeks, and would have been thoroughly investigated. But there was a sensible explanation for each of these inconsequential people, and that was good enough.

After each of Pigeon's attempts at talking to the spirit of the dead person, Roland followed a routine. First he gathered his tools from the Durango. Then he hauled a large burlap bag from the shed. He leaned a rake and a hoe against the corner of the house. It didn't matter where. He wasn't going to use them until much later.

No one ever stopped by. No one walked near enough to his property to really observe what he was doing, and since he saved these chores until nightfall, he was safe. But he laughed sometimes at his precautions. He had learned on the road how the presence of a few ordinary objects, of little interest to most people, could easily cast a different light on a scene. In towns up and down the coast, in those months before he came back home to stay, Roland had performed all sorts of "disappearing acts" in partial view of neighbors and strangers. Each time, he'd behaved with the natural air of a man going about his business, innocent and unconcerned.

His best trick, one he'd perfected and felt proud of, was making a loaded burlap sack appear lighter than it was when he hoisted it and headed for his vehicle. This was a bit of finesse during the removal, just in case he was seen. No one would question him so long as he appeared to be a man doing his job, raking up garbage, rocks, and debris and hauling it away. He stood upright. He didn't struggle or move too quickly. He wore coveralls in a bland color, and a bandana in his pocket or on his head.

Even now, at his current job, most people never noticed him. Most of the ones who did notice wouldn't acknowledge him. The few who acknowledged him couldn't recall his name. Every single time the office manager asked him for help, whether it was finding a ladder or changing a light bulb, the shriveled-up lizard had to read Roland's nametag to remember what to call him.

At work and at large in the world, he was no one. Only at home was he celebrated for being what he was.

He liked to garden in the evening, after supper. He enjoyed the unmistakable crunch of bones fracturing when he shoved a body into a more compact arrangement by stepping or sitting on it. He was a solid man, mostly muscle. He used burlap bags so the remains could rot and fertilize the ground.

This was the fate the dead deserved for failing his sister. More than that, he imagined their bodies served as an offering to whatever restless spirit lived in the earth, roaming under the soil seeking nourishment. Maybe, when it was satisfied, it would speak to Pigeon out of gratitude.

They were especially pleased with the way the actor turned out. Twisted into a semi-circle, he served as a sturdy anchor for Pigeon's latest birdfeeder. They didn't keep any animals, so birds were a particular pleasure for Pigeon, especially in winter. Any decent offering of food and water would attract an amazing variety. The actor helped keep the post steady, and when the season changed, his flesh would serve the sweet-smelling flowers with their blue-violet petals.

"He's just about the best one we've had," said Pigeon, beaming.

Roland used his own blend of fertilizer. The cow dung came from a farmer in Kelso. To this he added mulch containing grass clippings, dead leaves, and food scraps from the kitchen saved in a bucket under the sink. Later in the year he would plant the seed for the bluebells Pigeon loved so much. He had to agree the actor would serve them better than almost anyone.

In the meadow between their house and the dirt road, they had cultivated crimson bee balm and tassel rue. Roland had fed these mostly with the cut up remains of a woman he'd met at a tavern near Kalama. She was a saleswoman who drank too much and bragged about how good she was "in the sack." He remembered this while crushing her skull inside the burlap bag, and it made him chuckle.

The drunken saleswoman had carried an expensive laptop computer in a leather suitcase. These he'd buried at a construction site. She wore a gold necklace and matching earrings he probably could have pawned, but instead had tossed into a ravine.

He was proud of himself, proud of his habit of not coveting or keeping trophies. He remembered what he'd done. He didn't need trinkets to remind him. He only wanted the land to bloom with wildflowers and trees. He liked the hum of it, the wildness of bees and the kind of animals that didn't wreck what they touched.

Every place where human animals lived, the land kept dying away. The old man and his business friends and rivals had helped kill the forest. Over the course of Roland's life he'd seen the woods shrink to nothing but fringes beyond some half-hearted landscaping. He blamed the old man, but he also blamed the newcomers, people who drifted in and took what they wanted.

Brother and sister had never discussed their living arrangements. They never made rules. Pigeon cooked, and decorated the house any way she wanted. Roland helped her tend the garden and clean the house. He ran errands. He handled repairs. He turned over his paycheck every week, and accepted an allowance out of it for their household budget.

Their complicity had been forged in the locked tool shed, where as children they told stories of battles between ancient monsters, and invented games ("levitation" was a favorite) to pass the time and distract them from the growling of their bellies. Likewise, they had huddled together in the old man's truck every time they were told to wait there, stoically refusing to acknowledge a drunken mill worker masturbating on the passenger side window, or the well-dressed man who tried to coax them into unlocking the door, or the old woman holding up a dead rabbit for them to see and smiling like it was a chocolate Easter bunny no one could resist. They knew better than to trust these people because the old man had taught them suffering.

In all situations, their aim was for both of them to survive. This held until the afternoon, long ago, when Roland stood up to his full height and punched the old man in the gut. The shame of running away to avoid the consequences would last a good while. He carried it around with him for months, from one lousy town, one lousy job, to another—from Bellingham to San Diego and back. When there was no coastline left, he had seen Pigeon in his dream, leaning over him, calling to him, and he had returned home.

"Circle always comes back," Pigeon had told him on his first night home, after they killed the old man. He'd never had to ask forgiveness. She knew him so well.

The dream of a woman falling from a bridge: *arms wide and eyes watering from the stiff breeze; below, the currents churning up centuries of sand and glass and rotting wood; the woman's hair whipping from side to side; her smile vanishing the second she falls,*

knowing her true dimensions for the first time and measuring her life by the flashing light all around her.

The lanky girls liked to roam around in places where they didn't belong. Both took chances their parents probably wouldn't like. If someone had reported their little hikes and adventures, they would have been grounded.

That was what city parents did. They "grounded" their kids, or gave them "time out." It made Roland laugh. These lazy, overweight children sitting in a row outside the principal's office knew nothing dire was waiting for them on the other side of that door. The principal wasn't allowed to touch them, for fear of being sued. Their parents didn't punish them, because it might cause them some kind of emotional damage. And half of the kids were medicated for one condition or another—everything from allergies to narcolepsy. It was all such a joke, and the proof was right in front of Roland every day.

The two lanky girls liked mischief. At least, one of them did. She was having fun being a little bit bad, but it wasn't serious. The other one, the scroungy one who lived in the trailer park, was harder to explain. She was what the old man used to call "an accident waiting to happen." She had a sly way of hanging back, slouching in the shadows. She followed instead of leading, but everything they got up to seemed to be at her bidding, as though she willed it or somehow put the idea in the other girl's head.

Their favorite place to go was Odelia Farrow's cottage. The house was deserted and rundown. The yard was full of dilapidated windmills and garden decorations. There wasn't one thing of interest to any right-minded girl of thirteen or fourteen. This was another sign. Something drew them to the place. It could have been anything, but Roland decided it had a connection to the second girl, the strange one.

He couldn't get too close. They were skittish, always darting and whispering, watching over their shoulders for danger. Whenever he sensed they were on the alert, he staked out a spot and spied on them with binoculars.

The more he studied their habits, the more surprised he was by their friendship. Aside from their sloppy clothes and hair, they didn't have anything at all in common. One was the precious only child of a city couple, the Davises, living in a house Pigeon and her cafeteria co-workers called "the mansion," on a piece of land where a fire years ago had killed several residents and scorched the earth. People ought to have built an altar there, Pigeon always said, instead of an overpriced house with cedar decks and sliding glass doors.

"You mean like a place to say prayers?" Roland had asked. "Or like a place to speak to the dead?"

"No, not a place for people," she said. "A marker, to say 'something terrible happened here, and people should stay away.' No one should go there."

The dream of a boy suffocating: *hidden on a shelf of damp earth, hearing the night owl shriek; leaves rustle above the child's head, and the thing stalking him stops running, turns its face from side to side and sniffs the air.*

Roland saw the girls plotting at the library, but he decided not to follow them home again. Pigeon said she was having car trouble again, and begged him to get the problem squared away. He didn't mind giving her a lift, but they both knew it interfered with his activities, and with her freedom. Pigeon didn't need much, and what she did claim for herself was inviolate, so he resigned himself to the task at hand.

For most of the evening he played mechanic. After he got the car running, he gave it a standard check-up as well: oil, tire pressure. When he finished, the car was in fine shape.

The next day he kicked himself for losing sight of the lanky girls. Something had happened, a very bad thing, and this wasn't only a feeling or a suspicion on Roland's part. The news landed and then swept through Clark Middle School like a tornado.

Both girls would be absent from their classes that day, and the next day, and no one knew when they would return. The second girl, the scroungy, weird one named Briar Kenny, who lived in a trailer park near the freeway, had become the center of a tragedy. The previous week no one had known her name, and now everyone was talking about her.

The night Roland spent up to his elbows in motor oil and grease, repairing Pigeon's car, a fire had destroyed Briar Kenny's trailer home. She was being relocated to a shelter for people with nowhere else to go.

"This is it!" Pigeon said, when her brother relayed what he'd heard.

He didn't include the part about how he'd been following the girls for days. He hated to admit his fascination, since it hadn't led to anything practical, anything they could use. "This is what?" he asked.

"That shelter's another place where there ought to be an altar and not a house," she said. "At least, not a house full of people who don't know what it means."

Roland sipped his coffee and studied her face from the other side of the kitchen table. He and his sister had little in common, physically. He was broad-shouldered and solid, with close-cropped sandy brown hair and eyes the color of a Skillute mud puddle. Pigeon took after her mother's family, with dark hair and sharp, delicate features.

"What does the place mean?" he asked. He didn't bother asking how she knew. It was like all the other things Pigeon understood without consulting books or a computer, sometimes without even talking to people. Her true knowledge didn't come from gossip. It came from the land itself. Roland had no doubt that one day the dead would speak to his sister, and she would know their secrets.

"It means we have a better chance than ever before," Pigeon told him. "Come with me."

Roland didn't question her methods. In the basement he watched her pull on a loose-fitting coat over her housedress. "For travel," she explained. She wrapped a scarf around her neck and invited him to be seated behind the stainless steel table. He sat there waiting, as if he had a front row ticket to a grand performance.

"What should I do?" he asked.

"Not a thing," she told him.

"Do I need a coat?" he asked.

"No," she said. "You're staying right here."

"And not doing anything?"

"Right," she told him. "Be here in case anything goes wrong."

"Like what?"

"Oh," said Pigeon. "If I faint or anything."

"Are you going to faint?" he asked, suddenly worried for her safety, above all.

"I don't expect to, but who knows?" she said. "Now, stay as quiet as you can."

Pigeon took a deep breath. She placed her hands on either side of her head, like blinders blocking her peripheral view. Her eyes were open, and her breathing was slow and steady.

"Where is she? Where is she?" Pigeon asked. "The girl named Briar Kenny, where is she?"

Her eyes were open wide, peering at emptiness. If she had been outdoors, Roland would have assumed she was searching for something lost in the yard or the meadow, but there was nothing to see. It gave him shivers, just sitting there watching his sister in a coat and scarf, staring into shadows and darkness, whispering.

In the morning Pigeon was too exhausted to get out of bed. Roland took her a cup of tea with honey and lemon, her simplest and most favorite remedy. He sat on the edge of the bed and watched her drink.

"You want anything to eat? Toast?" he asked.

"I'm all right," she said. "I'll take a shower and head to work soon."

"How's the car running?"

"Good," she said. "All good, thanks."

"You're always welcome to ride into work with me," he reminded her.

"You know I like my Kenny Chesney private time," she said with a grin. "Just Kenny and me and the open road—all the way to work. I can just about get in two and a half songs."

"That's not much," he said.

"You'd be surprised what a difference it makes, though. I'm a lot nicer when I've had my Kenny time. Some days I don't even add vacuum cleaner dust to the mashed potatoes."

They laughed, because it was true.

"Sis?" he said. "What did you see last night?"

"Not much," she said. "Not enough. I mean, I could tell it was the girl, Briar."

"At that house, the shelter?" he asked.

"Yeah," said Pigeon. "I recognized her. I've seen her at school. She's got leaves tattooed on her neck. Last night she was lying in bed, raised up looking at me. Or maybe she didn't see me, but she was looking in my direction."

"Did you talk to her?" Roland asked.

"I tried," she said. "I kept trying, but the words wouldn't come out. It was almost like she was having a dream and I was in it, and she was the one who could talk, but she wouldn't speak to me."

Roland bowed his head. He wanted to help, and he wanted her to stop. Something felt wrong about all of this. He wasn't sure if it was what Pigeon told him or if it was this girl, the scroungy girl with leaves tattooed on her neck. What did they know about her, besides her name and what Roland had observed while following the girls every chance he got? They sat around acting sullen and moody in Odelia Farrow's garden. Why? One of them lived in the nicest house within ten miles, and one had lived in a trailer with her trashy mom and dad until it burned up. He could find out more, but he wasn't sure he wanted to know.

"Is this a good idea?" he asked. "I mean, trying to reach this girl?"

Pigeon's lips were delicately curved. She had a natural smile, a barely noticeable upturn at the corners of her mouth, as smooth as a rose petal.

"This is what we've been hoping for," she said at last.

Roland wasn't sure he'd been hoping for anything in particular. He couldn't imagine what it would be like if Pigeon got what she wanted. What if she broke through and spoke to the dead? What if they heard her and decided to answer?

"Are you happy?" he asked.

She smiled, beaming. "Yes!" She drank the last of the tea and climbed out of bed.

Once, while Roland was staying in a town called Munsville, in Oregon, he'd had a feeling something big was about to happen. He knew it in his bones. He drove along the main drag until he felt like stopping. He backed his truck into a space behind a restaurant that had gone out of business, and left the doors unlocked.

Pretty soon he could hear them. Two young men in jeans and cowboy boots were scuffling with a middle-aged man in the alley.

Roland saw them punch and kick the guy. They wrestled him to the ground. One sat on his legs while the other tied his ankles together. They stuck something in his mouth and tied his wrists. Then they rolled him into a doorway, and Roland lost sight of all three.

He crouched down and ducked his head. It was early November and the alley was littered with maple leaves. The air smelled like dirt and rain. He didn't know what he was waiting for. If one of the younger men came at him, Roland could pick him up and shake the life out of him. Things might be different if both of the men rushed him.

He caught sight of a dust cloud in the air from the young men as they scrambled out of the doorway and ran off. They were long gone before Roland reached the guy.

In no more than a couple of minutes, those two had made a pulpy mess of the guy's face. Three of his fingers pointed at wrong angles. He couldn't talk around his broken front teeth, but he groaned like a dying mule. The man was so busted up, so close to giving up and dying anyway, Roland climbed back into the truck and drove off.

He had wondered, ever since, what the sensation was that drew him to the alley. It wasn't anything he'd seen. It wasn't anything he'd heard. None of the men were people he had ever met before. He didn't even remember the name of the restaurant. So why had he been there? Could he sense blood, the way animals smelled fear on their prey?

Thinking about it now, on his way to work, Roland came to the conclusion he must have detected some sign, a real thing, a physical clue. Any other explanation was no longer acceptable. Pigeon was the one with the ability, if anyone in his family had it. She was the one, and it was only fair to let her use her gift if she could.

All day Roland stayed busy. He checked and re-checked cleaning supplies. He made the trash rounds twice. He took a leaf blower to the parking lot. Then he spent a few hours preparing herbicide and spraying it on the cottonwood trees on the periphery of the campus. There was no explanation for all the soft white fibers in the air so early in the season. He had never seen anything like it before.

In the halls he kept an impassive expression. He pretended not to hear kids gossiping about what had happened to the girls who were out of school, or about Tyler Blanchard, whose mother had reported him missing.

Roland was the only person who knew about the hallway scuffle between the girls and Tyler, the only person who could connect them. As far as anyone knew, the boy must have run away. Most people would make all of the assumptions Roland expected, and if he said nothing, the boy would just be one more mystery in a world of lost creatures.

The aroma of meatloaf greeted him as soon as he started up the front steps. He changed clothes in his room and joined Pigeon in the kitchen. She was sitting at the maple wood table reading an Eddie Bauer catalog.

Roland set a bottle of jasmine cologne on the table in front of her. She snatched it up and carried it to the back door. She went outside to spritz and sniff, and came right back with a big grin on her face.

"This is a really nice one," she said.

Roland gave her a wink. She appreciated the little luxuries and goodie bags he brought home.

Kids were so spoiled. The things they threw away or left behind in the bathrooms and the locker room at the gym would fill a department store counter—not only cologne and powder and unwrapped packets of scented soap, but cashmere sweaters, silver earrings and, surprisingly often, cash. He had to make a show of turning in most of the valuables, things like phones and watches, to Lost and Found in the administrative office. Anything he passed along to Pigeon, she couldn't wear at work, but she didn't mind at all. Thanks to his thoughtful efforts, her bedroom was brimming with sweet-smelling products they couldn't otherwise afford.

They had lived in this well-built house together since they were born. Roland couldn't imagine a home like the place where Briar Kenny had lived before the county sent her to the shelter. He thought she was better off there. For one thing, the girl's parents were animals. He'd seen what they did, while the girl was running around the countryside with her friend. They didn't even close the curtains.

Roland's house was built for good people, and some of the people who had lived in it had been good. His grandfather had added some fine touches to it. Everything they could possibly want was right under their noses. The old man's savings from the lumberyard weren't hard to claim. Roland found the money in a safe at the back of his closet, all cash. Not enough to live on, long-term, but enough for the upkeep on the land.

The house was well made, a holdover from a time when craftsmanship mattered. Plenty of newer houses had collapsed. Sitting empty, after being stripped of plumbing and any fixtures worth a dime, most were gutted and knocked down. Recently a brand new realtor had appeared, and was buying up lots as fast as tenants could be persuaded to move. Nobody knew what would soon take the place of the crummy neighborhood where Briar Kenny had lived with her animal parents.

Roland wasn't much interested in the troubles of people who were scavengers or who were just passing through, but he hated the way they scarred the land for no good reasons. They took up space, and they took advantage of the "country prices," but they didn't leave anything worthwhile when they finally gave up and moved on.

Some of the lots cleared for construction around Skillute were nothing but vacant ruins. Not enough people who wanted to live there could afford the new houses, and the developers weren't interested in building homes for regular working people. Meanwhile, on all sides stood the miserable, ramshackle houses of the poor, some of them wiped out after an illness in the family or lost income, others new to town. Despite their poverty and lack of skills, they kept arriving, spilling over from nearby cities, desperate for a break they were never going to find in a place like Skillute.

They couldn't afford even the cheapest apartments closer to Portland or Seattle. They took lousy part-time jobs cleaning trailers and RVs, washing windows, or mucking out the stalls at one of the stables owned by horse trainers and breeders. No matter how they tried, they never moved up, because there was nowhere to go. They had come to the country thinking life would be easier, but they didn't know the first thing about living off the land. In the end, Skillute was just like the places they'd left behind. Well-to-do people with trust funds and jobs they could perform long distance got the good houses and the good life, while the poor got nothing.

Roland routinely saw houses with all the lights out, knew they were occupied, and reckoned they were late on their electric bill. Not even a porch lamp shone along some streets.

A mile from Roland's home, a whole block of houses stood empty, surrounded by weeds and decimated woods. Every acre in this part of Skillute had long ago been stripped back, and the trees cut down and shipped to paper mills in Tacoma. It didn't even smell like the outdoors here anymore. The air was heavy with the scent of auto exhaust and gasoline. A fine black dust wafted down from the freeway overpass, mingled with the unseasonal cottonwood fluff, and clung to the walls and doors and roofs below.

"Be very quiet," Pigeon said. She was dressed as she had been the previous night, in a coat and scarf—her "traveling clothes." Candles flickered along the basement walls. Roland sat before her, silent as she commanded.

This time she took a minute to breathe and relax. She rolled her head from side to side, loosening up. She shook out her hands and jiggled her fingers. Then she closed her eyes.

Seeing her like this, Roland felt a flicker of fear again, a sense that some element of her plan was misguided. But he had no idea how to say these things.

The candle flames danced, sending shadows up and down the walls. In the cold basement there was only the sound of Pigeon's voice, murmuring.

"Where are you? Briar Kenny! Let me see you. Let me see."

Her head turned slightly left and right. She was scanning, searching with her eyes closed.

"There!" she said. "There you are."

Her head was still, her inner gaze fixed on someone Roland couldn't see.

"Come on…" she whispered. "Come on, girl… Get up!"

She reached both arms out. Her hands clasped the air.

"You don't want to crawl through a nasty, filthy chimney!"

Roland stared at the empty space before Pigeon. He noted the way her hands remained loosely clenched, as though she held another person's hands, guiding them.

"All you have to do is look at a window and take a step…"

She let go and dropped her arms at her sides. "Hear them singing?" she asked.

"Who?" Roland whispered, but she didn't hear him.

"Ah!" She put her head back.

"Pigeon," he said. She didn't acknowledge him.

"Witches!" she said. "Witches!"

She held her head back, eyes closed, and smiled broadly. A film of crimson gore spread across her teeth and dripped down onto her chin.

For the first time in months, Roland dreamed all night. He was inside the Durango, parked at an intersection. Across the street he could see houses, trailers, and tin-roofed shacks all jumbled together. The walkways were mud paths and there were no doors on any of the dwellings, only screens.

He was about to start the engine when he saw them. The two lanky girls came loping across a scruffy backyard, ducking down close to the ground, weaving and climbing like cats.

There was some confusion at the back of one house. Roland heard the squeal of rusty hinges on a screen door. A shout went up. Then all hell broke loose.

First the screen squealed again and swung wide. A woman stumbled out and fell onto the ground. From the back of the house a man was screaming. The woman jumped to her feet and ran. She was down the street, hauling ass, her hair flying, when all of the lights popped on and people came spilling out of the dwellings, which were now tents and wooden crates stacked on top of one another.

The screaming reached a fever pitch. The high wail broke off and flames burst through the sides of one tent after another. From somewhere inside, a person crawled out, burning, half-awake, half-dead, dragging across the ground, flesh bubbling and bursting in the heat. The dying person collapsed on the asphalt, arms reaching for help.

Roland felt his throat closing. His lungs struggled against the smoke and heat, and he woke gagging, dry heaving against the bedclothes.

When they were children, Pigeon and Roland had learned a poem from Pigeon's mother, Sophie. It was a singsong kind of verse about a little orphaned girl who moved in with a family, and who did the mending and the cooking and swept the hearth clean. The orphaned girl did all the things a woman ought to do around the house, but there was something wrong with her. She liked to scare the children with her tales of demons and ghosts. More than that, she was a magnet for terrible things. Evil recognized her somehow and drew closer like a moth to a wicked flame.

After her mother absconded, Pigeon liked to tell the story over supper. She told it when the old man left them in the tool shed, and when he left them locked in the truck. She must've told it five hundred times. She never got tired of it, and Roland pretended to like it. He pretended he wasn't afraid, until finally the fear went away.

"What happened?" he asked Pigeon over coffee. "What happened last night? What did you see?"

After her latest adventure, Roland had done the same thing he'd done the first time. He caught Pigeon before she collapsed, and carried her to her room, where she slept heavily the rest of the night.

She was paler than usual in the morning, with deep circles under her eyes. Her slender hands were unsteady when she sipped from the mug and placed it on the table.

"Skillute," she said at last. "I saw the town, the way it was and the way it is now. I saw people who lived here before us, and I saw people we know."

"Who?"

"You remember those kids that used to sneak around the tool shed?" she asked. "The ones you scared off with the shotgun?"

"The creeps?" he asked. "Brother and sister, always looked like they were starving?"

She nodded.

"They disappeared, back a few years ago," he said.

"Disappeared," she repeated. There was no expression to her voice, and it made Roland's skin crawl.

"Sis," he said. He had to take hold of her hands to make her look at him. "I don't know what happened to those kids."

"Somebody does," she told him.

"Who does?"

"That girl," she said. "The one at the shelter. Briar Kenny. Only..."

"Yeah?"

"She's not right," said Pigeon.

He wanted to agree. He wanted to tell what he had seen while following the two lanky girls. But then he would have to admit how much he'd kept secret from the one person he ought to confide in.

How could he ever tell her all the things he'd learned from the old man? He shared what he thought she needed to know. She didn't ask him many questions. They had always been this way.

His mother, for example, and Pigeon's mother—"the absconded." He knew the truth. He had stood by while the old man buried Pigeon's mother in three of the planters where they now grew strawberries. Roland had heard the sound of the shovel blade cutting the soil. He'd stood to one side, watching, and then he'd helped to cover the holes.

First the old man had separated the body into two sections and cut the head loose. The dark hair splayed on the mound of earth, eyes and mouth open, gaping. She had been a fairly pretty woman, in her youth.

Roland had done as he was told. His stepmother was already dead, and nothing he said or did could change a thing. Up to that moment he had believed the story of his own mother running away, stealing fifty dollars from the old man to buy a bus ticket, leaving all of them to rot. Watching the old man shovel the moist dirt into that once pretty mouth, and eyes, and hair, changed his view.

From then on Roland had only been biding his time, waiting for a chance to escape. When his time came, he ran as far as he could, but even that didn't work out. Night after night, for months, on the road and in one miserable little town after another, he kept imagining Pigeon's face—eye sockets empty, lips twisted and covered with dirt.

He'd put everything at risk to return. It was still the only real thing, the only purely good thing he had ever done.

"What's wrong with the girl at the shelter?" he asked.

"Something," she began. She stopped, glanced out the kitchen window. The morning air was so full of cottonwood fibers, it looked like snow falling. "Something's inside her. And it might be our fault."

"I don't get what you're saying," he told her. He had already missed his chance to shower before work. Soon he would have to call in sick. He couldn't leave Pigeon like this.

"We've been feeding it all along," she said. "We've kept it going, and now it's inside that girl. I tried to tell her. I tried, but I wasn't strong enough."

"You're saying you talked to her? Where she is right now? In that place?"

"She spoke to me," said Pigeon. "She followed me, and I almost had her. I almost had her."

"Where?" he asked.

"On the rooftop," she said. "I had her out on the roof, and she was ready. I was about to tell her to fly."

"You mean jump?"

"I mean fly," she said. "Like all of those tiny bits of fluff in the sky. I told her they were witches."

"Witches?" Roland shook his head.

"I was hoping she might jump, if she thought she could fly," Pigeon said, and he could see that this made perfect sense to her. "We were together, and if she jumped while I was there, everything would come true, Roland, you see?"

He did see. He saw his sister, shattered so many times and put back together. He saw himself standing beside the old man with a shovel, ready to pour the earth over the only person who had ever been kind to him, and not shedding a single tear for fear of what the old man might do next. He saw himself as a baby, shivering in his mother's arms. Who was she, and how desperate, to marry the old man and live under his terms? Who was Pigeon's mother, if she came here to live and to nurse another woman's baby? What kind of woman did that? What kind of person would accept the old man's attention, and let him keep a roof over her head, if she had a choice?

"I know," Pigeon said.

"Know what?"

"I know what you and the old man did," she said. "I know what you buried under the strawberries."

Roland had never taken a vacation or called in sick. He only showed up at the school that morning to tell Jody, the manager in the administrative office, he was taking a few days off to look after his sister, who needed minor surgery. This not only gave both of them the time they needed, but elicited a lot of whispered sympathy from Jody.

"Oh, tell Ava we're all so sorry. Take all the time you need," she said. "We can put a couple of detention students on trash collection and cafeteria cleanup, it'll do them good. You know, my mom had hip replacement surgery last year, and six months ago my brother had an appendectomy. Of course both of them called *me*. I'm the sibling who shows up and takes care of things, you know? I'm the one who makes sure their bills are paid and their plants are watered. I should've been a nurse or a physical therapist, you know, some kind of healer."

Roland thought of a blue heeler when she said that. He couldn't get it out of his mind, after. Jody's face, voice, even her name would be forever linked to the image of a cattle dog.

"We have your current phone on record, right?" she asked. "In case any questions come up."

He checked the number. "We're good," he said.

"Is this a *landline*?" Jody asked, although it was none of her business. All they needed was a contact number.

"Yeah," he said.

"I don't remember the last time I met anyone who didn't have a cell phone!" she said.

"Well, now you have," he said. "We're behind the times. My daddy was the old-fashioned type."

"The Apple store at the mall is running a special," she told him.

Roland had never considered buying a smartphone. To his mind it was nothing but a fancy tracking device. They had two TV sets, but no cable service. He paid his bills on time. The house belonged to him, and he paid taxes in February every year. For groceries and household supplies, he paid in cash. He didn't own a computer. If he wanted to check anything online, he used a computer at the school library. He avoided memberships, and wasn't fooled by giveaways. He'd bought the Durango used, from a guy in Longview who'd advertised with a cardboard sign in his driveway.

"Okay," he said to Jody. "I'm going to be pretty busy for a while, but maybe we'll think about it." He edged out the door to the office and got out of there as fast as possible, avoiding any more unwanted attention.

Pigeon wasn't having an operation, but she was in a bad state. Every time he took her a sandwich or soup or a cup of tea, she sat up in bed and accepted gratefully, but she didn't show any restless signs of recovery. She only slept or read magazines or gazed out the window at the sky, where she said she was watching dead children play.

Roland was convinced that her illness—or whatever this was—had come from her contact with the girl at the shelter. He'd been right all along about her, the scroungy girl from the trailer park. Briar Kenny was an evil influence. Pigeon believed the girl had been lured and taken over by something that was now living inside her, acting like the girl but also consuming her. At least, that was what Roland was able to make of her words.

Days passed. When Pigeon was strong enough to heat her own meals without help, Roland told her he had business to take care of and he might be gone overnight. He filled a rucksack with protein bars and pop-top canned food. He packed all the tools he thought he might need. He left his sister with a well-stocked kitchen, clean sheets, and a loaded shotgun.

The girl had left the shelter and moved in with her friend's family. So now both girls lived under one roof in the Davis home, the "mansion" with cedar decks and sliding glass doors. No matter how Roland turned this over in his mind, it could not have occurred by accident. It was too much to think that a scroungy girl with brown leaves tattooed on her neck had moved up from a dumpy trailer to her friend's luxurious home purely by chance.

Behind the Davis house the earth was arranged in neat, semicircular terraces. Nothing wild ever grew here now. The yard was as carefully shaped and managed as the house.

Cottonwood fibers floated through the air. They shimmied lightly like snow flurries.

Roland staked out the house from an outer terrace. He didn't like to risk being spotted in case the girls recognized him, and he liked the sensation of cool air surrounding him. He crawled forward and lay low, edged forward again and lay on his belly, watching the house with binoculars. The ground beneath him was flat and cold and he wasn't aware of drifting off, lowering his head to rest on the damp leaves and gently falling asleep.

The dream of Roland, the same dream he dreamed, lying on the ground: *owls hooted in the dark and rolled their magnificent eyes. In the branches and twigs beetles trundled along, dragging their prizes of plant stems and earthworms. Down the road a dog barked, a hearty loud woof every three seconds, eventually dying away on the cold air.*

Roland stood in the dense forest and craned his neck, up and up, to the vast ceiling above. A sliver of night sky penetrated the treetops, appearing and disappearing when the uppermost leaves swayed. Nearby a triangle of cedar shingles marked a spot overtaken by moss and slugs.

An L-shaped house nestled in the cedar and Douglas fir. A large catalpa grew beside the back door. Inside, the lights were on. A woman was humming a tune.

A man in hunting clothes sat on the ground with his back against a tree trunk. He held a shotgun across his knees. He was crying silently, his heavyset torso wobbling with each breath.

A pregnant woman sat on the back steps of the L-shaped house. She skim-tossed one stone after another into the woods, and then lit a cigarette. The smoke curled in loops overhead and faded away.

Tracing where the loops had been, all the way back down, an invisible spiral ended not in the L-shaped house, but in the "mansion" with its oversized windows. They shone like silver, reflecting the moonlight behind the cedar decks.

The back door to the house crashed open. Three female figures came spilling out—one who must have been the Davis woman, and the two lanky girls, Briar and the Davis girl, who were dressed for bed, layered in pajamas and robes. Briar wore slippers, and a coat over her pajamas. The Davis girl stumbled about in woolly socks.

They were shouting, but not at Roland. The girls were arguing, punctuating their words by shoving one another.

"You're a liar!" the Davis girl screamed. "You're a liar!"

"Get back inside the house!" the Davis woman yelled. "Get inside right now!"

This was when Briar pulled a knife from her coat pocket. She held it up like a hunter, admiring the clean blade.

Shivering in the cold, the Davis woman rose up, and suddenly she seemed larger, arms spread, shielding her daughter from Briar. She shouted the names of both girls.

While she was struggling, Briar lunged with the knife and the Davis woman let out a scream as the blade entered her abdomen. Swift as a darting bird, the girl pulled the knife back, and a viscous stream of crimson came pulsing from the wound onto the ground.

All three were screaming, the Davis girl trying to reach her mother. Roland was caught off guard, frozen, mesmerized by the blood soaking into the snow-white fibers on the ground, and forming an arc where the woman fell.

Roland woke up. His breath formed a vortex of condensation. He blinked and pushed himself up off the ground. Every muscle in his body ached.

It was morning. Birds called above. Roland watched them chase one another across the bare open sky. He realized he could be seen, and dropped back down to the ground.

Gradually he made his way along the top garden terrace, crawling until he found a better position from which to keep watch over the front door. The windows were too dark to afford a view of the interior. This spot was his best bet for keeping track of who came and went. It wasn't ideal, but it was better than the place where he had slept for several hours.

As he tracked back through his dreams, he could recall every detail. The fragrance of every leaf and the crackle of twigs and undergrowth were as vivid as the yellow catalpa and the emerald moss on the cedar shingles. It was more like a hallucination than a dream.

He wondered, briefly, if he might have been having a vision of some kind, a warning of what was to come, but he didn't believe that. None of his experiences had ever seemed other than real to him. Pigeon was the one with the gift of sight or speech, if it existed. Lately he had begun to doubt this, too. Maybe all of her attempts at talking to the dead were nothing but family legends wrapped up in the need to feel special, to have one thing she could call her own, one thing neither the old man nor Roland had given to her, and the world couldn't take away.

While Roland was thinking of all that his sister had done for him, all the ways she made his life possible, and wishing he had more to offer her, he saw a silver-haired woman dressed in black, with a black trench coat, walk up to the Davis house. He had to use the binoculars to locate her car. Obviously, she was hoping not to be noticed here. It might have been because she was afraid of something, but Roland couldn't guess what that might be.

He was waiting to catch a glimpse of Briar, the wicked girl, and he had in mind what he would do to her as soon as he could draw her out of the house. But why would anyone be afraid of either girl, or of the Davises? They appeared to be typical city transplants, getting more bang for their buck in a town where prospects for most people were uncertain. They probably had jobs that allowed them to work from home, and salaries large enough to afford not only the "mansion" but also a gardening service and new vehicles.

When the Davis woman opened the door to the silver-haired lady, Roland waited. The Davis woman and the silver-haired lady went inside.

When the girl emerged, sneaking as usual, closing the front door precisely so as not to make any noise, at first Roland couldn't tell which one she was. It seemed as if the two had become more alike, or maybe they were only dressing alike. This one, the Davis girl, wore sloppy jeans and a faded T-shirt under her jacket, but there was no tattoo on her neck. She crept away from the house until she reached the road, and then bolted.

Roland let her go. He was waiting for the other one, Briar, the bad one who was making Pigeon sick. Whether she was a witch or a demon or a person twisted into something evil, he wanted her gone. He had plans for her, plans he should have carried out the first time he saw her and felt the strange signals in the air around her.

He rummaged through the supplies in his rucksack and ate a protein bar. Then he took a swig of water from his thermos. He swished the water around in his mouth before swallowing.

Whatever the silver-haired lady and the Davis woman were doing in there, they were taking their own sweet time. He was starting to think his whole approach might be wrong. It might have been better to just knock on the door, force his way in, and do away with all of them.

This last thought had to be a result of too much sleep and not enough to eat. It had seldom crossed Roland's mind to go after more than one person at a time. The risk had to skyrocket, and the outcome was far from certain. No, this was going to take patience.

The dream of darkness: *fetid heat, the close and stifling proximity of a dead body; pain in every limb; a taste of blood oozing inside the mouth; slipping under and suffocating in the black, silent emptiness.*

An hour later, the silver-haired lady had still not exited the Davis house when the second family vehicle pulled into the driveway. A man Roland took to be Mr. Davis unlocked the front door and walked right in.

"Shit," Roland said out loud. The situation was getting worse, and he had no idea what people like this did in their spare time. For all he knew, they might be hosting a party. He imagined five or six more cars showing up, full of smartly dressed couples bearing gifts of food and wine. Someone would turn on loud music. People would dance on the lawn. Just what he needed, a house full of city people seeking entertainment.

Before he could get his mind around this possibility, Mr. Davis exited the house and hurried to his car. Roland hadn't used the term "burning rubber" in quite a while, but it definitely applied to the way that guy peeled out of the driveway and headed down the road.

He waited. There was no sign of the silver-haired lady. No sign of anything but the drifting cottonwood. And then it all started.

The front door was not so much opened as flung wide. The Davis woman stepped onto the welcome mat and made sure her husband was gone. At least, that was the explanation Roland seized upon. Whatever she was doing, she didn't want her husband to see it.

Fortunately she was bold about the rest of the world's scrutiny or she would have spied Roland on his belly, lying at the farthest edge of the garden's top tier. His gray clothing blended well enough with the landscape, and he had further camouflaged himself using the cottonwood fluff scattered everywhere. But if she had been just a bit more careful, she would have spotted him.

She propped the door with a large rock and the welcome mat. She reached inside the house and grabbed hold of something with both hands. When she leaned back and began hauling it out, Roland almost gave an involuntary shout. His jaw hung open for a few seconds, and he reached for the binoculars.

Up to this moment he had been unaware of the small, low-roofed shed behind the house. He had picked it up in his peripheral vision, but he had no reason to pay attention to it. The structure afforded no surveillance of the comings and goings of the family, and it would have been an uncomfortable hideout.

Now he was keenly aware of the shed as he watched the Davis woman drag the inert body of the silver-haired lady—dead or unconscious, he couldn't tell which from this distance—from the house to the shed. There she used a key on the padlock. She grabbed the lady by one ankle and pulled her inside. Roland heard the unmistakable sound of wood crashing onto wood as she moved things around, making space. When this was over, she emerged from the shed but didn't lock it. She went back to the house and went inside.

In her bedroom, Pigeon opened her eyes. She sat up in bed. Outside the cottonwood flew rampant and thick. If she didn't know better she would have thought, at first glance, that there was a blizzard underway.

She checked the clock on her nightstand and found it had stopped at noon. She jumped out of bed and ran downstairs. She put on her coat as she hurried to the basement. Her only hope was that her brother would hear her warning and come back before something terrible happened.

Roland lost all sense of his purpose in coming to the house when the Davis woman came outside again. She struggled less this time, for the heavy-duty garbage bag she was dragging was lighter in weight than the silver-haired lady. From a tear in the bag a foot protruded, sheathed in a sock. The shoe was missing.

Roland had no thought to control his reaction. From his hidden position flat against the ground he rose to full height and stared as the Davis woman shoved the body in the garbage bag into the woodshed, slammed the doors shut, and replaced the padlock.

"Fuck me," he said.

The woman was turning toward the house. At the utterance of those two words, she stopped. Then a moment passed in which anything might occur. A meteor might hit the ground between where she stood, frozen, and where Roland stood at the top of the garden terraces. Birds might fall from the sky. An earthquake might shake the house to its foundation. Anything and everything could happen.

She turned toward him. It was more of a pivot, as if she could tell exactly where he was by listening or by sniffing the air. And when she faced him, her eyes registered everything about him in one glance, as though she recognized him. Almost as though she had been waiting for him, instead of the other way around.

He was cold and alert, but not afraid. The murderer before him, if she were the murderer and not her husband, was a slender woman of about forty with no visible weapon. He had seen her dispose of two bodies, but he hadn't seen how they died.

If he had faced another enemy, another man or a woman with a gun, he would have fled. He could have jumped over the cement blocks bracing the back wall of the garden. He could have outrun most people, and he could surely take most people in a hand-to-hand fight. Knowing this, he stood his ground.

In the basement of their home Pigeon faced one direction after another, trying to sense her brother's presence. She searched with her eyes closed, and she called his name. No matter which way she turned, the feeling was the same. She could find nothing. Certain this was their only hope, she opened her eyes, took a deep breath, and began again.

The Davis woman was walking toward him. Not rushing, and not moving slowly, but climbing the terraced hill as steadily as if she were strolling up to examine the flower beds and not the man standing on top of them. The disarming thing was the way she never took her eyes off him, not to check her footing and not to see if anyone was watching.

Instinct propelled him forward. If his bulk and his willingness to rush her could frighten her off, he might get out of the situation undamaged.

By the time she reached the middle section of the terraces, she was sprinting. Thinking he could use her momentum against her, Roland came hurtling down the hill, crushing and toppling plant support cages and miniature trellises on the way.

He slammed both her shoulders with his fists and sent her toppling backward. She landed on her head and her body followed slowly, at pendulum speed, with a sickening crack.

Roland skidded to a stop on the lower terrace, his boots sinking deep in the soil. Overhead the air was choked with cottonwood fluff, swishing in every direction like the white flakes in a shaken snow globe.

He took another step toward her body. Her head was cranked viciously sideways, and her arms and legs splayed in various directions. He froze when he heard the cracking sound again. His mouth opened and wouldn't close when she whipped her head around into its normal position and stood up. Her arms shivered and shimmied until they fell into place. She tossed back the hair that had fallen across her face and started walking toward him again.

The howl that erupted from the woodshed sent ice through Roland's veins. The Davis woman seemed surprised, more so when the shrieking from the shed was accompanied by a loud banging noise. One of the bodies in the shed wanted out, in a bad way.

The woman raised her eyebrows and laughed. It was a low, mean chuckle that reminded Roland of the old man whenever he hurt one of the children and knew they were fighting back tears—seeing them cry was his greatest pleasure, because it gave him an excuse to hurt them again. The subsequent pain would be much worse, and the old man would offer it by way of a lesson in stoicism.

"Are you crying, little baby? Do you think anybody in the world's gonna take pity on you just because you curl up in a ball and cry?"

Roland would shake his head, no. No, he would not cry. No, he wasn't expecting pity from anyone, not ever. In his head, he would answer the questions: "Fuck, no. Fuck, no, you fucking bastard!"

Even as a small boy, he was wise enough not to voice the words. But thinking them gave him courage to endure what was coming.

The shed erupted again. This time the sides shook, and the top kept popping like it was going to explode.

With a couple of minor adjustments, the Davis woman was back to her normal appearance. She never stopped staring at Roland.

"Hey, big boy," she said. "Is that all you've got?"

She ducked her head, clenched both arms, and rushed at him. This time she opened her mouth wide, and a roar like a grizzly caught in a trap came shrieking out of her.

His natural inclination kicked in once more. He lunged at her and they crashed, all four feet leaving the ground at the same time. In mid-air she swung at him with both fists and punched the sides of his head. When they landed, he toppled over, holding both ears and wailing.

She reached for him. He rolled backward and kicked his feet as high as he could, lifting her into the air and sending her flying. She skidded all the way down the hill, with leaves and cottonwood clinging to her.

Another howl from the shed split the air. The woman staggered to her feet and rushed Roland again. This time he rolled to the left and tripped her with his feet. She hit the dirt hard enough to knock out a linebacker. In a second she raised herself up and started to stand.

In their basement Pigeon stood with both arms raised. Her eyes rolled back in her head and she plunged into darkness, chanting wildly.

"Allow me into the darkness, let me in..."

Roland only heard the Davis woman scrambling to her feet. In that last second before he could turn away, she grabbed hold and broke his left arm. He lay crumpled on the ground, every instinct telling him to protect himself. Agonizing arrows of pain shot through the left side of his body. But he knew if he turned inward and tried to crawl away, it would only make her stronger.

He got to his feet and shambled toward her. With his right hand he grabbed her by the throat, shook her, and lifted her as high as he could. She was wailing like a wounded animal until he snapped her neck. With a mighty shove and a grunt of pain, he hurled her into the terrace, where the cottonwood surrounded her like flower petals.

He didn't run. He wanted to, but some power held him to the spot. Before anything else happened, he needed to be in motion again, heading toward the tree line. He needed to clear it and keep going. He needed to escape, to survive. Nothing else mattered now. Still, he was stuck, and couldn't take another step.

He saw the Davis woman's body lying among the trellises. There was no movement other than a slow, steady seeping of blood into the cottonwood. The howling and smashing inside the shed had stopped.

Roland felt a shadow fall across him. In a small heap on the terrace, something was lying bent and broken, its limbs twisted like those of a forgotten doll. Out of the corner of his eye he noticed a pale outline flickering between the sparse trees. He tried to track the movement, but it was gone, a mere distraction.

The next blow landed like a boulder tossed by a giant. The Davis woman's entire body crushed against his chest, knocked him down, knocked the wind out of him and sent shockwaves through his left arm. The radius and ulna were shattered and the flesh hung limp, flattened against his torso.

He heard her breathing hard behind him. On his belly and with only his bruised legs and one arm, he tried to drag himself toward the house. If someone arrived, or if someone drove down the road right now, they might see him. None of this would be good. Nothing he said would exonerate him. But he might live.

He was aware of blood, only vaguely sure it was his own. It mixed with saliva and dripped from the corners of his mouth. When the next blow landed in the center of his back between his shoulder blades, he heard the crunch before the pain registered. He put out his right hand, tried to stretch it to full length, but some of his ribs were broken and the extension caused everything in his chest and abdomen to shift and grind horribly. He retched. He vomited with his face only an inch above the dirt.

"Fucking," he muttered.

"Excuse me?" the woman said, her voice perfectly normal in pitch and tone.

"Fucking bastard," he said, husky with phlegm.

"I'm not sure what you mean, but I have to change clothes and get ready for dinner. You're holding me up," she told him.

He let loose a gravelly cough. It was all he could manage.

"I have other things to do, obviously," she said, nodding in the direction of the shed. "She can't fool me."

"Fuck," Roland said, grimacing, trying to propel his body without enough bones and muscles to do the job. He growled. He spat blood and vomit at the ground in front of his face. It clung to his lips. He tasted dirt, ashes, and the dry cottonwood. He moved his tongue up and down, but the fibers only stuck to the inside of his mouth and with every movement it shifted further down his throat. He tried to heave it up, but there wasn't enough saliva to make it go either direction.

He gagged and vomited again when the woman lifted his shoulder with the toe of her shoe and rolled him over. He lay there face up, choking. Blood ran from his nostrils.

He was aware of being dragged, dirt and gravel catching in his hair and in the skin on the back of his neck. He heard the rattle of the padlock, and a scream followed by a thud. Then he was being dragged again, into the dark, into the space where he'd spent so much of his life before he'd had the nerve to kill the old man.

He was lying on top of the wood and the bodies of the silver-haired lady and the trailer park girl. It was dry inside the shed. The smell of cedar was intoxicating. The last flash of sky disappeared with the rumble of the padlock.

There was a crunch of footsteps on earth, walking away. The Davis woman—or whatever this creature was, whatever its name might be—was done with him and was leaving him here to die.

Beneath him the silver-haired lady was cold, and she smelled faintly of lavender. There was something else nearby, something warm—broken and warm.

He tried to breathe, tried to think, but all of the words and images spun around him. He wasn't able to catch a single clear idea. His brain was on fire, as overheated as if he had a fever from the flu. Some words kept popping up, and his lips tried to repeat them.

"Hear," he said. "Hear. Here, to me."

This wasn't it. He was choking, blacking out.

"Hear me."

The voice wasn't his. He stopped trying to speak, stopped fighting the clot of cottonwood bulging in his throat. He let his eyes close. He felt all of the pain and all of the desire to escape falling away. The darkness enfolded him, and whatever was keeping him alive sank into the ground. He lay like this, shrouded in an infinite peace, for some time.

And then it began. In the cold, dry darkness of the shed, he became aware of words, dreamlike, whispered, moving over his body, searching for him...

"Roland."

It was not a dream. It was his sister's voice, as clear as if she lay beside him.

"Brother," she said. "Hear me."

He kept his eyes shut tight, and in the pitch black an outline formed. He could see Pigeon leaning over him, reaching down to caress his cheek as she had done since they were children. He smelled the sweet aroma of her honeysuckle soap, and a strand of her dark hair fell across his face.

"Roland," she said. "Hear me. Take my hands, now. Take my hands."

He clenched his right hand, and it closed gently around hers. He drew a breath and felt his lungs expand. He opened his eyes and she was there, wiping the tears and blood away, leaning down, her eyes looking into his.

"Roland," she said. "Come home."

Acknowledgments

Thank you to my husband for everything. Thank you to Trepidatio and my wonderful editor, Scarlett R. Algee. It's been an honor and a privilege. Thank you to Sean Leonard for sharp proofreading and great suggestions. And thanks to everyone who's read and taken to heart these strange tales of Skillute.

S.P. Miskowski is a recipient of two National Endowment for the Arts Fellowships. Her stories have been published in *Supernatural Tales, Black Static, Identity Theory, Strange Aeons* and *Eyedolon Magazine,* and in numerous anthologies including *The Best Horror of the Year Volume Ten, Haunted Nights, The Madness of Dr. Caligari, October Dreams 2, Autumn Cthulhu, The Hyde Hotel, Darker Companions: Celebrating 50 Years of Ramsey Campbell, Tales from a Talking Board* and *Looming Low.*

Her second novel, *I Wish I Was Like You,* won This Is Horror 2017 Novel of the Year and a Charles Dexter Award for Favorite Novel of 2017 from *Strange Aeons Magazine.* Her books have received three Shirley Jackson Award nominations and two Bram Stoker Award® nominations, and are available from Omnium Gatherum Media and JournalStone/Trepidatio.